Paul O. Zelinsky grew up with a picture of Hansel and Gretel standing hand in hand before a house made of cake and candy, with dark forest all around. The painting was by his great-grandmother, and he used to look at it and wonder about the brother and sister lost in the woods.

Now his own oil paintings bring to life this most compelling of childhood tales. They depict a world as real as our own—tactile, colorful, detailed, conveying the elemental emotions of the story without sweetening or dilution. Rika Lesser's spare retelling, based on the tale's first transcription by Wilhelm Grimm (1810) and its first appearance in print (1812), perfectly complements the rich, vivid storytelling of the art.

HANSEL AND GRETEL

HANSEL
AND
GRETEL

Retold by Rika Lesser

Illustrated by Paul O. Zelinsky

A TRUMPET CLUB SPECIAL EDITION

ISBN 0-590-31672-9

12 11 10 9 8 7 6 5 4 3 2 1   7 8 9/9 0 1 2/0

Printed in the U.S.A.   14
First Scholastic printing, September 1997

AT the edge of a great forest there once lived a poor woodcutter. He could scarcely manage to feed his wife and his
two children, Hansel and Gretel, and this made him
miserable. The day came when there was nothing left to eat in
their house but one loaf of bread, and he grew terribly anxious.

His wife said to him that evening as they lay in bed, "Listen, Husband, there is something you must do if we are not all to starve. Early in the morning, take the two children, give them what little bread we have, and lead them into the forest. Build a fire for them, and while it is burning, go away and leave them there alone." For a long time the man could not reconcile himself to his wife's plan, but she would give him no peace until he finally agreed.

The children had heard everything their mother had said, and Gretel began to cry. "Hush," Hansel whispered. "It will be all right. I have an idea." Then he got up as quietly as he could, put on his jacket, and went outside. White pebbles on the ground glistened in the moonlight.

Hansel carefully gathered them up and stuffed the pocket of his jacket with as many as would go in. Then he went back inside, lay down beside his little sister, and fell asleep.

Early in the morning, before the sun had risen, the parents came and awakened the children. To each one they gave a little piece of bread. Gretel took both pieces and put them under her apron because her brother's pocket was filled with pebbles. Then they all set out on the path into the forest. While they were walking along, Hansel often stood still and peered back at their house. His father said, "Why are you always stopping and looking back?"

"Oh," Hansel replied, "I am looking at my white kitten, who is sitting on the roof and wants to say good-bye to me." Secretly, however, each time he gazed back, Hansel dropped one of the small white pebbles on the path.

The boy's mother said, "Just get going! That's not your kitten. It is the morning sun shining on the chimney." But Hansel kept gazing back and each time he did, he let another stone fall.

And so they went on walking a long time, until they were in the midst of the great forest. There they stopped and gathered firewood. Their father lit a huge fire, and when it was burning brightly their mother said, "Rest a while now, children. Your father and I are going off to cut wood. Wait here by the fire until we come back."

The children sat by the fire and ate their bread. They waited until nightfall, but their parents did not return. When it grew very dark, Gretel began to cry; but Hansel said to her, "Wait just a little longer, until the moon is up."

And when the moon was up, the white pebbles gleamed in the moonlight and showed them the way. Hansel took Gretel's hand, and together they walked all through the night. In the morning they reached home. Their father rejoiced to see them, for he had not been happy about what he had done. But their mother was angry.

Not long after, again there was almost nothing to eat in the house. And again, after going to bed, the children heard their mother tell their father that he must take them into the forest, deeper than they had gone before. And again Gretel began to cry. And again Hansel got up very quietly to go out and gather pebbles. But when he got to the door, he found that his mother had locked it. Hansel, too, grew sad and could not comfort his little sister.

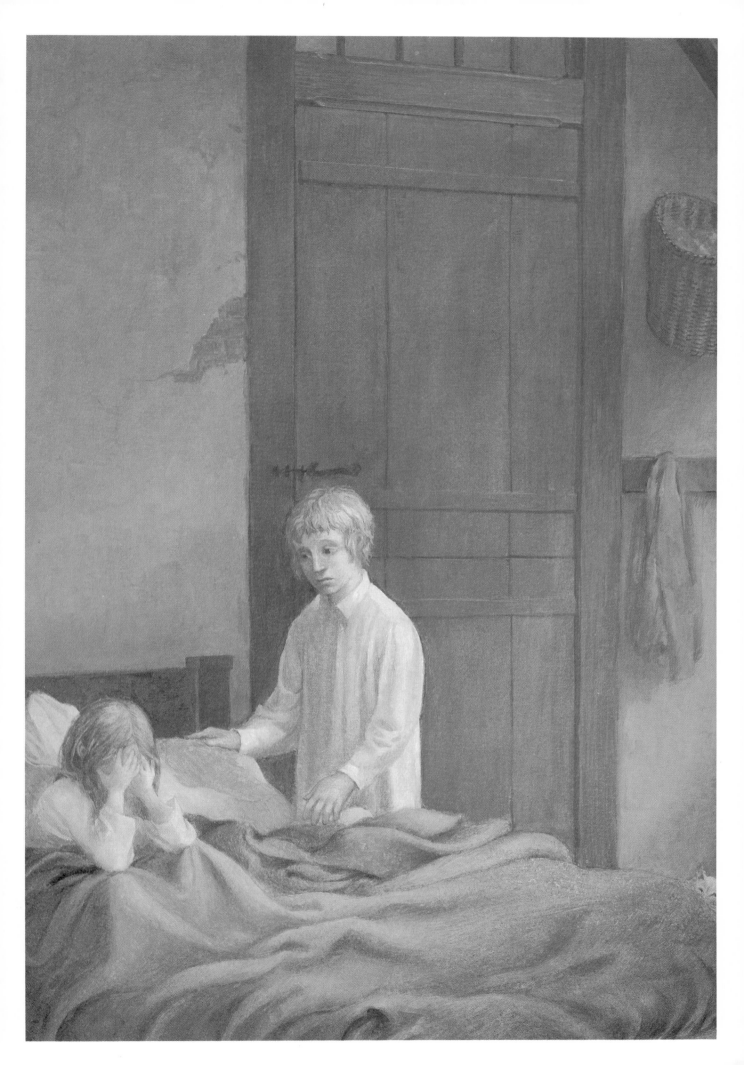

Early in the morning, before daybreak, they all got up, and each of the children was given a small piece of bread. As they walked along, Hansel often paused and gazed back. His father asked, "My boy, why are you always stopping and peering back at the house?"

"Oh," answered Hansel, "I am looking at my little pigeon, who is perched on the roof and wants to say good-bye to me." Secretly, however, he had crumbled up his bit of bread, and each time he turned around, he would drop a crumb on the path.

His mother said, "Just keep going! That's not your little pigeon. It is the morning sun striking the chimney." But Hansel kept glancing back and each time he did, he dropped another crumb.

And when they had come even deeper into the forest, to where it was thickest, they stopped. Their father built a huge fire. Their mother told them to rest and wait while they went off to chop wood. As they sat by the fire, Gretel gave half her bread to Hansel, for her brother had strewn all of his along the path. They waited until evening, but no one came to fetch them.

When it grew very dark and the moon rose, Hansel looked for the bread crumbs. But they were gone. The thousands of woodland birds had pecked them up and eaten them. Hansel still meant to find the

way home and he pulled Gretel along after him. They walked all
through the night and all the next day, but they were lost in the great
forest.

On the third day, chilled and hungry, they came upon a little house that was built out of bread. Its roof was made of pancakes and its windows of sugar candy. The children were so happy to see it that they ran up to it, Hansel to the spongy roof and Gretel to the sparkling panes of the window. And they ate greedily. Hansel was devouring

a huge chunk of the roof and Gretel was pushing out yet another windowpane when they heard a thin voice call out from inside:

"*Nibble, nibble, nubble! Who gnaws my house to rubble?*"

The children were so frightened that they let fall what they had in their hands.

Just then, a gnarled old woman came gliding out the door. When she caught sight of the hungry children she wagged her head and said, "Oh, you poor little things, come along with me! There's plenty to eat *inside* the house. I'll take good care of you." And she took them both

by the hand, led them inside her house, and served them a fine dinner.
Then she made up their bed and the tired children lay down and fell
fast asleep.

The next morning, before Hansel and Gretel were awake, the old woman crept up to their bedside. As she watched the two of them sleeping so sweetly, she thought to herself, "Now there's a tasty morsel for you!" And she lifted Hansel up and carried him outside and locked him up in a little stall, as if he were a piglet. Then she went back inside and shook Gretel awake, yelling, "Get up, you lazy girl! Go out to the well and draw water and then get to work and make something good to eat! Your brother is in that stall over there. First we are going to fatten him up, and when he is fat I will eat him."

Gretel was terrified of the old woman and had to do as she was told. Every day she brought Hansel water and lots of good food to eat; she herself got nothing but crayfish shells. And each day the old woman went to Hansel's stall and told him to stick out one of his fingers so she could feel if he were growing plump. And each day Hansel held out a bone instead of a finger.

One evening, after four weeks had gone by and it still seemed that Hansel was growing no fatter, the old woman said to Gretel, "Now be quick about it, go out and fetch water to fill the cauldron. Tomorrow morning, whether or not your little brother is fat, I am going to slaughter and boil him. While you are getting the water, I will be kneading dough. We'll bake bread while he's cooking."

Early in the morning, when Gretel got up to light a fire under the cauldron full of water, the bread was already in the oven. And the old woman called out to Gretel, "Come over here right now! It smells as if the bread will soon be done. My eyes are weak; I want you to look and see if the bread is turning a golden brown. If you can't see in far enough, then get on this board and I'll push you in. There's plenty of room in the oven. Once you're inside you can take a good look."

Now the old woman really meant to leave Gretel in the oven to roast. But Gretel could tell what the woman had in mind and said to her, "I'm not quite sure how to go about it. Could you show me? If you get on the board, I'll push you in."

And the little old woman sat on the board and Gretel pushed her into the oven as far as she could. Then she slammed the door and fastened its iron bolt. Inside the oven, the old witch screamed and howled. And while Gretel was running away, the old witch burned to ashes.

Gretel ran directly to Hansel's stall and let him out. She told him what she had done, and the happy children hugged and kissed one another.

One last time they went back inside the witch's house. Everywhere they looked were precious gems and sparkling jewels. They took all

they could carry with them and set off for home. They walked and
walked, and at last the woods began to look familiar.

When they arrived home, their father wept with joy to see them. Their mother had died, he told them. Every day that they were gone had been filled with sadness.

Now they emptied their pockets of the glittering jewels, and the woodcutter and his children lived happily and prospered to the end of their days.

Storyteller's Note

"Hansel and Gretel" was one of the first oral tales the Brothers Grimm collected. The original storyteller, a member of the Wild household in Kassel, told it to Wilhelm. His handwritten transcription of this tale bears the title "Little Brother and Little Sister." It was included among the many tales the brothers collected, annotated, and sent to Clemens Brentano (German poet, dramatist, and collector of folk tales and poems) in the autumn of 1810. When the brothers published their first edition of the *Children's and Household Tales* in 1812, they lengthened and stylized this tale and called it "Hansel and Gretel."

There have been numerous later editions of the *Grimms' Tales*, seventeen supervised by the brothers themselves. But the storytelling here more strongly invokes the 1810 and 1812 Grimm versions (as they appear in German in Heinz Rölleke's critical edition of *The Oldest Collection of Tales by the Brothers Grimm*, 1975) than it does any of those they published later in expanded, revised, and stylistically embellished forms. It is not a translation of any one text.

Some English readers may miss the familiar rhyme: "Nibble, nibble, little mouse, / Who's that nibbling at my house?" which is commonly given for the German, "*Knuper, knuper, Kneischen! / wer knupert an meim Häuschen?*" "*Kneischen,*" generally taken as a nonsense word, is one diminutive form of the word "*Knaus,*" and it exists in more than one German dialect. In the context of the witch's house, it quite plausibly means the knoblike, crusty swelling on a loaf of bread, which arises where one loaf has stuck to another in baking, and is here rendered as "nubble."

Rika Lesser

Rika Lesser is a poet and translator of German and Swedish literature. She is the author of *Etruscan Things* (The Braziller Series of Poetry, 1983), and is known for her translations of Rainer Maria Rilke's poetry and Hermann Hesse's poetry and tales. For both her own poetry and her translations she has been the recipient of several grants and awards, among them the Amy Lowell Poetry Traveling Scholarship, an award from the Ingram Merrill Foundation, and the Harold Morton Landon Translation Prize from the Academy of American Poets. She is on the faculty of the Poetry Center of the 92nd Street Y in New York City and lives in Brooklyn, New York.

Paul O. Zelinsky is a painter who has illustrated a number of distinguished books for children. He is the author and illustrator of *The Lion and the Stoat,* and the adaptor and illustrator of *The Maid and the Mouse and the Odd-Shaped House* (Dodd, Mead), one of *The New York Times'* Ten Best Illustrated Children's Books of 1981 and *School Library Journal's* Best Books of the Year. Among the many other books he has illustrated are *How I Hunted the Little Fellows* by Boris Zhitkov (Dodd, Mead), an ALA Notable Book and one of *SLJ's* Best Books, 1979, as well as *Ralph S. Mouse* and *Dear Mr. Henshaw,* both by Beverly Cleary. He lives with his family in Brooklyn, New York.

The artist and writer have known one another since their undergraduate days at Yale.